DANIEL TIGER'S NEIGHBORHOOD™

Friends Help Each Other

adapted by Farrah McDoogle
based on the screenplay "Friends Help Each Other" written by Wendy Harris
poses and layouts by Jason Fruchter

Ready-to-Read

Simon Spotlight
New York   London   Toronto   Sydney   New Delhi

SIMON SPOTLIGHT
An imprint of Simon & Schuster Children's Publishing Division
1230 Avenue of the Americas, New York, New York 10020
This Simon Spotlight edition July 2014
© 2014 by The Fred Rogers Company All rights reserved.
All rights reserved, including the right of reproduction in whole or in part in any form.
SIMON SPOTLIGHT, READY-TO-READ, and colophon are registered trademarks of Simon & Schuster, Inc.
For information about special discounts for bulk purchases, please contact
Simon & Schuster Special Sales at 1-866-506-1949 or business@simonandschuster.com.
Manufactured in the United States of America 0614 LAK
2 4 6 8 10 9 7 5 3 1
ISBN 978-1-4814-0366-5 (pbk)
ISBN 978-1-4814-0367-2 (hc)
ISBN 978-1-4814-0368-9 (eBook)

Hi, neighbor!

Today I am playing

with Katerina Kittycat.

"Meow, Meow!
Do you want to have a
tea party?"
asks Katerina.

"Let me get a chair for you!" says Katerina.

"No, thank you," says Katerina.

"I can do it all by myself."

Oh no!

Katerina bumps the table with the chair.

Everything falls on the floor!

"What happened?"
asks Henrietta Pussycat.

"I made a mess,"
cries Katerina.

"Our tea party is ruined!"

"Maybe Daniel can help!" says Henrietta.

"Teatime!"

says Katerina.

"I want to pour the tea by myself!"

Oh no!

Katerina spills the tea.

I can help clean up the tea!

Friends help each other, yes they do!

"Do you want to pour more tea?" asks Henrietta.

"Yes! But this time
I will not do it
all by myself!" says Katerina.

Yes!

Friends help each other,

yes they do!

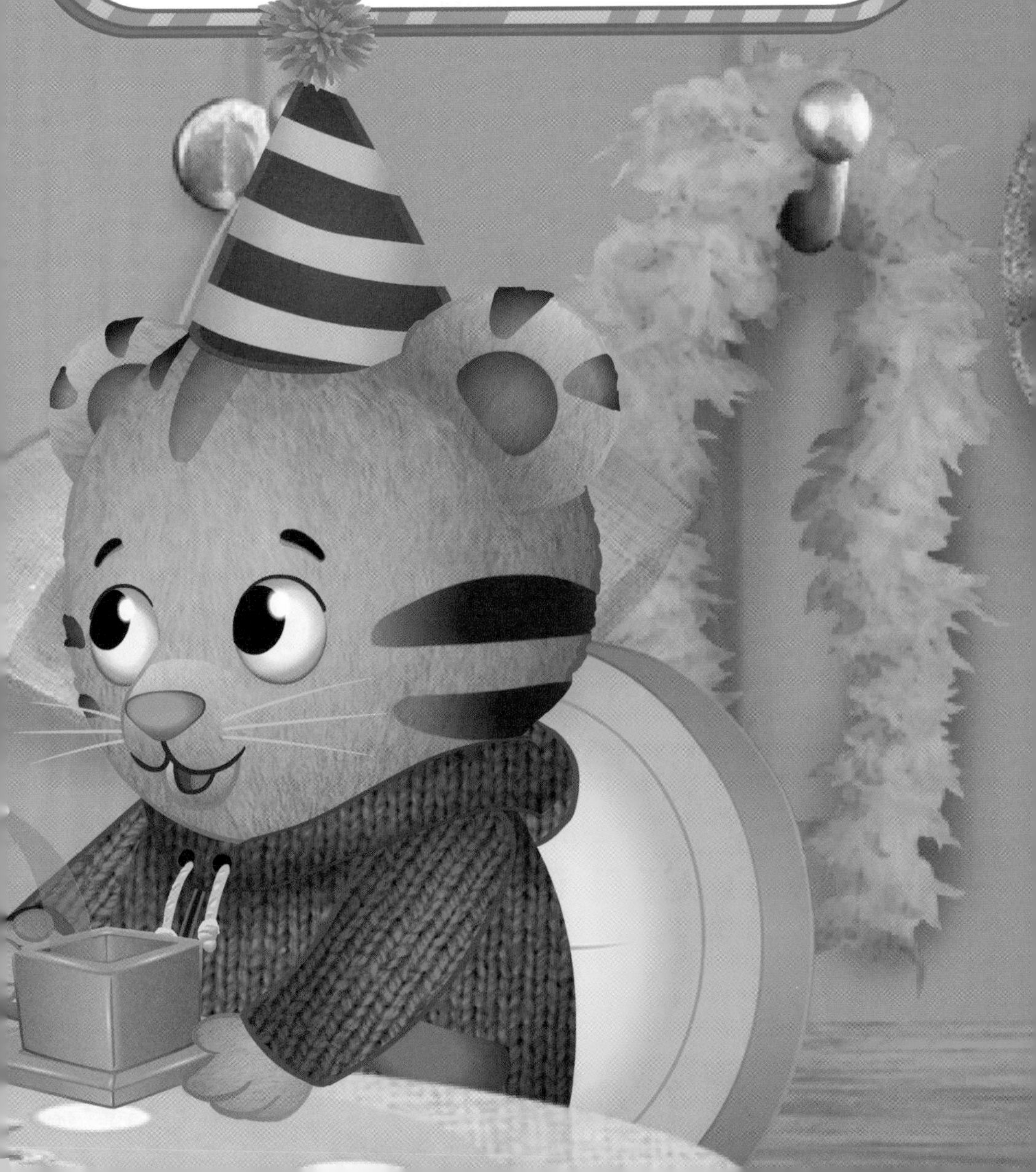

I am happy I helped
my friend today!
Ugga Mugga!